PIG GETS LOST

This is Apple Tree Farm.

This is Mrs Boot, the farmer. She has two children called Poppy and Sam, and a dog called Rusty.

Mrs Boot has six pigs.

There is a mother pig and five baby pigs. The smallest pig is called Curly. They live in a pen.

Mrs Boot feeds the pigs every morning.

She takes them two big buckets of food.
But where is Curly? He is not in the pen.

She calls Poppy and Sam.

"Curly has got out," she says. "Please come and help me to find him."

"Where are you, Curly?"

Poppy and Sam call to Curly. "Let's look in the hen run," says Mrs Boot. But Curly is not there.

"There he is, in the barn."

"He's in the barn," says Sam. "I can just see his tail." They all run into the barn to catch Curly.

"That's not Curly."

"It's only a piece of rope," says Mrs Boot. "Not Curly's tail." "Where can he be?" says Poppy.

"Let's look in the cow shed."

But Curly is not in the cow shed. "Don't worry," says Mrs Boot. "We'll soon find him."

"Perhaps he's in the garden."

They look all round the garden but Curly is not there. "I think he's lost for ever," says Sam.

"Why is Rusty barking?"

Rusty is standing by a ditch. He barks and barks.
"He's trying to tell us something," says Poppy.

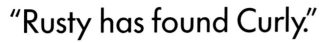

"Rusty has found Curly."

They all look in the ditch. Curly has slipped down into the mud and can't climb out again.

"We'll have to lift him out."

"I'll get into the ditch," says Mrs Boot. "I'm coming too," says Poppy. "And me," says Sam.

Curly is very muddy.

Mrs Boot picks Curly up but he struggles. Then he slips back into the mud with a splash.

Now everyone is very muddy.

Sam tries to catch Curly but he falls into the mud.
Mrs Boot grabs Curly and climbs out of the ditch.

They all climb out of the ditch.

"We all need a good wash," says Mrs Boot.
"Rusty found Curly. Clever dog," says Sam.

First published in 1990 by Usborne Publishing Ltd. Usborne House, 83-85 Saffron Hill, London EC1N 8RT Copyright © Usborne Publishing Ltd. 1996,1990